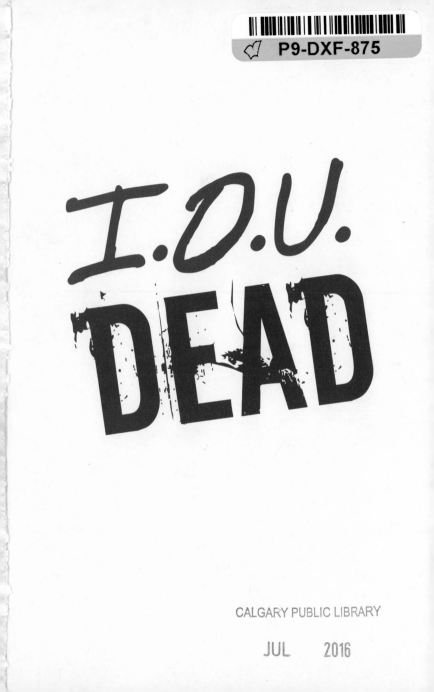

I.O.U. DEAD

I.O.U. DEAD

MICHELLE WAN

RAVEN BOOKS
an imprint of
ORCA BOOK PUBLISHERS

Library and Archives Canada Cataloguing in Publication

Wan, Michelle, author
I.O.U. dead / Michelle Wan.
(Rapid reads)

Issued in print and electronic formats.
ISBN 978-1-4598-0908-6 (pbk.).—ISBN 978-1-4598-0907-9 (pdf).—
ISBN 978-1-4598-0909-3 (epub)

I. Title. II. Series: Rapid reads
PS8645.A53168 2015   C813'.6   C2015-901554-5
C2015-901555-3

First published in the United States, 2015
Library of Congress Control Number: 2015934283

Summary: In this work of crime fiction, Keno a bill collector is
unwittingly drawn into a murder investigation when he witnesses
a serial killer fleeing the scene of a crime. (RL 4.0)

*Orca Book Publishers is dedicated to preserving the environment and has
printed this book on Forest Stewardship Council® certified paper.*

Orca Book Publishers gratefully acknowledges the support for
its publishing programs provided by the following agencies:
the Government of Canada through the Canada Book Fund and the
Canada Council for the Arts, and the Province of British Columbia
through the BC Arts Council and the Book Publishing Tax Credit.

Cover design by Jenn Playford
Cover photography by iStock.com

ORCA BOOK PUBLISHERS
www.orcabook.com

Printed and bound in Canada.

18 17 16 15 • 4 3 2 1

To Mary, a good and wise friend.

ONE

My name is Keno, and like my name, my life is a lottery. I'm twenty-three and I'm a collector. I don't mean stamps or baseball cards. I chase up skips and deadbeats, people who don't pay their rent, people who run out on their bills. It's not a nice job. I feel sorry for a lot of my targets, who, when I catch up with them, always have a sad tale to tell. But some are pretty shifty. A few you wouldn't want to meet without armed backup.

When I was a kid, the doctor told my mom I was ADHD—attention deficit hyperactivity disordered. That means my mind wandered, and I couldn't sit still. I also had a reading disability. Kids made fun of me because I stuttered under pressure and acted weird. I was what my teachers called *challenged*. I still am. But if there's one thing I am not, it's a bully. I hate bullies.

In case you're wondering why a guy like me thinks anyone would be interested in his life story, let me tell you. It's because someone's got to know. I want you to know what happened to me, and I don't have much time. A killer is out there on the loose, and before the night is out I may be dead.

TWO

They say every story has a beginning, a middle and an end. I see I've jumped you right into the middle. For you to understand what's going on, you have to go back with me. To the beginning.

The beginning is a typical night. Jaco gets his foot in before the Shadow can slam the door. He follows the foot up with his body, enough to let him grab our target and yank him out. Then Jaco jerks him in close.

"You can run, but you can't hide," Jaco says. "We'll always find you. You owe two months' back rent on your last address, and you're in arrears here. We've come to collect." He doesn't raise his voice, but you know he means business. He's bigger than me—I'm six feet in my socks—and ten times as mean.

The Shadow starts blubbering about how he ain't been paid, like it's his boss's fault he did a midnight flit out of his last place. And the place before that. We've chased this guy all over town. It's why we call him the Shadow. Jaco has him by the collar now and is banging him against the wall. He says, real sweet, "So let's do a deal. You pay up now, and I don't break your head." He gives the Shadow a harder slam when he says *head* to show he's serious. I wince.

The Shadow screams, "All right, all right. Just don't hit me again."

Jaco looks at me, all innocence. "Did I hit him? Did I strike our friend here?"

I shrug.

The Shadow is sniveling. He promises to have the money next week.

"*Now*," says Jaco. "Or that wall's gonna feel a lot harder."

"Okay, okay." The Shadow digs his wallet out. He gives us everything he has, still a few hundred short of what he owes. I write out a receipt, and Jaco says, "The rest tomorrow, or things are gonna get *real* intense. And don't even *think* about leaving town."

It's Jaco's standard routine. He'd rather beat the rent out of you than evict you, because eviction is messy, you have to serve notice, and most times you have to call the bailiff in. Usually the tenants are so mad they trash the place before they go—that is, if it can get any trashier. And he has no mercy on skips like the Shadow.

Still, I feel kind of sorry for the guy.

"You bashed him pretty good," I say as we walk out to Jaco's car. I zip my jacket up. These fall nights can be cool.

"He had it coming," Jaco says.

I remind him that we're not supposed to damage the clientele.

He snorts. "Don't waste your sympathy on that scumbag. For all you know, he's the serial killer the cops are looking for."

I do a double take and try to make out if Jaco's serious. It's hard to read his expression in the fading light. Most of the streetlamps in this part of town are out.

"Fits the profile, don't he? A loner, always on the move, looks harmless. But he's the kind who would sneak up behind you and *whack*!" Jaco makes a fake lunge at me. Now I know he's taking the mickey. All the same, the thought gives me the creeps. Two women have been battered to death in the past few months, and the city is on high alert. The cops have given the killer a name on account of his weapon of choice: the Hammer.

———

I've been at the job six months, Jaco six years. Some of what we do is regular rent collection for landlords. A lot of it is chasing down skips like the Shadow, who try to duck their debts by moving around. Most of the time we work our territories separately, but tonight, thinking about the Hammer, I'm glad we're paired. True, so far he's only attacked women. But you never know.

In fact, our work brings us up against some pretty mean characters. And slippery ones. That's when we work in twos. Jaco doesn't like being hitched to a Talkover like me. That's what he calls me. Anyone can talk over me. He's too smart for that, is Jaco. He's seen it all. It's probably what soured him on life.

Our next call is a duplex on Freeman. Her name is Amber Light—no kidding, it's really her name, which makes you wonder what *red* and *green* stand for with her. A cute redhead, always a couple of months behind and swift to dodge the rent man. I only met her once for that reason, but it was enough for me to know she's a real sharp lady. I was on my own that time, so she gave me her whole life history. Married young, divorced, old mum sick in Windsor, a wannabe actress working as a cocktail waitress until she gets her big break. Like so many people, she has her eyes on the prize and is barely scraping by.

"You're pretty enough to be an actress," I told her. "You should be in movies."

She just laughed. "I'm working on it, Mr. Kalder." She's the only one of my targets ever to call me Mister Kalder. Most call me names I wouldn't want to repeat.

"Well, work on having your back rent next time I call," I said, "or we'll be having a different conversation."

You see why Jaco calls me Talkover.

Tonight we're in luck. We catch Amber just as she's coming out the door. Her hair's all done up, and she's wearing dangly earrings, four-inch heels and a short, tight skirt that makes you look a dozen times.

"Ooh, fellows," she coos. "I know why you're here. Listen, I'm in luck. I got an opportunity like you wouldn't believe."

"Hot date with a Hollywood producer?" I say.

She grins. "Sort of. Listen, I mean it. I'm onto something big, and I'm late, so don't spoil it for me, okay? If things go right, you'll have the money next week, plus maybe even a little bonus for you. Promise."

She's real excited, and the way her eyes are dancing tells me maybe things are finally coming right for her. But Jaco isn't having it. He knows her kind too well. He starts to get tough, but I pull him aside and say, "Leave it."

9

"What?" He's unbelieving. "You know how many dud calls we've made on this number already? Slippery as a fish. When you hook her, you reel her in."

"Give her a chance," I say. "She may be moving up in the world."

I'm relieved when he walks back to her and says, "This time next week." But he says it in a way that means business.

She mouths us a kiss. "You're sweethearts, both of you." And then she's past us and down the walk, leaving a trail of spicy perfume on the air and getting into her old blue Corolla.

We finish the night with a few more calls. A drunk who wants to punch us out. A woman with a rottweiler who always gives us a hard time but who pays on the nose. A gorilla who owes a whack for a load of power equipment he bought last June, but no one's answering there. We check out the back. The windows are dark, and the place is locked up tight. We write it off as another dud call. Chances are fifty-fifty the bird has flown.

It's now past nine. I haven't had supper. I'm beat because I've been on my feet all day. I need food, and I need to hit the sack. I should explain. Our hours are when we figure people will be home. First thing in the morning, at the end of the day, and evenings or odd hours for folks who work shifts. Today was all of those. For sliders like Amber, it's important to know their schedules. Our targets have a sixth sense for when we're coming, so it's always a game of hide-and-seek. Jaco and I mainly work the inner-city zone—grim apartment buildings and run-down houses. Places that are only standing because they're too tired to fall down, where people live because they can't afford better. Most of them are just poor. Some are shifty. A lot look ground down. You got to feel for most of them. But, like I said, a few you don't want to tangle with unless someone has your back.

We grab burgers. Jaco wolfs down two and drives us back to base with our day's take. Base is Beaton Enterprises, over on Newlands Road, a street of mom-and-pop stores, pawnshops and fast-food joints. Cass, the secretary, sits in the front room with her phone, computer, filing cabinet and spider plant. She keeps the books, traces skips and does what we call the make-nice calls. These are to folks who creditors have given up on but who might respond to one last polite reminder before they're turned over to Jaco and me. A surprising number are high-end purchasers—cars, boats, supersize plasma TVs—some living in swank neighborhoods. We get all kinds.

How should I describe Cass? She's pretty in a serious sort of way, but I get the impression she's not happy with her life. I know this because she's always changing her hairdo.

One day it's in a ponytail, the next it's swept off to the side, another it's curly like a sheep's. Happy women don't do that. She's also trying to lose weight. I don't see how—she's always chewing caramels, stores them in her cheeks like a chipmunk. And she's always trying to improve things. I like to believe it's because she doesn't have a man, who I think ought to be me, but she's not having it.

She works the same weird hours as we do. It suits her because she goes to community college three days a week. I never made it through high school, and like I said, I have this reading disability. I think Cass is pretty smart—her face is always in a book. Jaco calls her Chipmunk Cheeks. He doesn't like her, but I think it's mainly because she's Mr. Beaton's niece. *His* office is on the right, through a door that's always shut. Far as I can tell, he lives there. I've never known him not to be around. On the left is what we call the counting house, where Jaco and

I tally up our take. It's a closet more than a room, with a table, a calculator, two chairs and a coffeepot always on the stew.

Cass is reading the paper when we walk in. She looks up. Her face is pale. "Another one!" She shoves the front page at us. "Battered to death. No woman's safe anymore. This male-on-female violence is the sign of a sick society." She says stuff like *male-on-female violence* and talks about what she calls *the cycle of poverty and abuse*. She gets it from her sociology class. She's doing a paper on crimes against women, and she almost makes it sound like it's somehow *our* fault.

Jaco holds up his hands and goes into the counting house, where he pours himself a mug of liquid tar.

To calm her down, I take the paper from her and check out the headline article.

"Read it aloud," she says. At first I think she's drilling me again. When things are slow, she sometimes tries to help me with

14

my reading by making me read things out loud. Believe it or not, my writing's not so bad. With writing I can choose the words. Reading, you never know what they'll throw at you. I have to focus hard. The letters dance around, and sometimes I have to take it syllable by syllable.

But she says, "Read it aloud so *he* can hear it." She shoves her chin in Jaco's direction. No love lost there.

I squint at the page. *"The body of a 32-year-old woman identified as Janet Short was found in her apartment early this morning by the building sup—sup"*—I know the word but have to squeeze my eyes shut to get the letters to behave—*"superintendent, who noticed Ms. Short's door partly a—a—"*

"—jar," Cass finishes for me.

"That means open, dumbbutt," Jaco calls over his shoulder.

"Shut up," I say. "I knew that. And don't call me dumbbutt."

"Ajar," Cass repeats, impatient with our bickering. "Found in a pool of her own blood. Time of death between 7:00 and 9:00 PM last night. Over in the Brentwood area." Hoo boy, she practically knows it off by heart. She leans back in her chair to call to Jaco through the door, "That's your beat, isn't it?" Even though it's sometimes my beat too.

"Not guilty," says Jaco. He's entering our day's take in the rent book. "Old Keno here can vouch for me. With me every minute of the time in question, hey, Keno?"

But I'm still reading. This third murder is true to form. Female victim, home alone, no struggle, similar cause of death—*blunt force tra*—I squeeze my eyes shut again—*trauma*. Blows to the head and body from something like a hammer. No weapon found on premises. And no witnesses. The killer came and went, and no one saw him.

I put the paper down.

"Hey, Talkover?" Jaco prompts me. "Had your eye on me all the time, didn't ya?"

"Yeah," I say. He's only sending Cass up. It's true we were together for the beginning of last night, because we were chasing sliders. Our technique is, one of us covers the back exit, and that includes windows, while the other goes to the front door. That's why you need to work in pairs. But for the rest of the evening we were collecting from regular paying tenants, so we split up, and no, I didn't have my eye on him the whole time.

The door behind Cass opens and Mr. Beaton comes out. He's bald, built like an ex-heavyweight, with pouchy, tired eyes. Don't let that fool you. Those eyes see everything. I'll Beat On You, we call him.

"Well?" he growls.

"Thirty," Jaco mutters, meaning we got money from 30 percent of the targets we visited, or one in three. In our line of work that's not bad, but it's not good either, because our take is a commission on what we bring in. Jaco's cut is more than mine because he's been on the job longer. I hardly make enough to pay for rent and food.

Beaton isn't happy. He gripes, asks what kind of turkeys are we. Every other collection agency is doing way better than us. We should be in the eighties, every late payment is money in the bank for the target, money out for him, yadda yadda yadda. He leans on us because *his* clients, the retail creditors and property owners—a lot of them slum landlords—are leaning on *him*. Beaton Enterprises is just the chase-down agency. Our job is to squeeze dollars out of persistent deadbeats, skips and stubborn defaulters. Guys like Jaco and me are at the bottom of the food chain. Beaton makes sure we know it. His nickname for us is the Two Bagels, because our names both end in *o*. As in *zer-o*.

THREE

I can't tell you how many jobs I've had. I've worked in car washes and supermarkets and dollar stores. I've shifted refrigerators, sealed driveways, cleared brush, rolled turf. I'm especially good at anything that needs a bit of muscle but doesn't require a lot of training or concentration. I'm not stupid. I have a lot of what my mom called native intelligence. I wish you could've met my mom. I wish she was still alive. She was a good person, always a kind word and would give you her last dollar if you were in need.

But what I'm trying to say is, of all the jobs I've had, collecting is the worst. I don't like the hours, the clients or the pay. I don't like what I do—screwing money out of people, a lot of them who really don't have it. Maybe it's their own fault. Maybe they blow it on drugs or booze or gambling or whatever. But when Jaco and I collect, especially from single moms, there are always kids crying in the background, someone going hungry or wearing ratty old runners to school. I'm also not crazy about Jaco, and I know he's not exactly nuts about me, so I guess we're even there.

Who I really dislike is the boss, Mr. Beaton. He tries to act like he's some kind of big business tycoon. We mostly collect for individual landlords, small developers and like that. But—and this may surprise you—also for some big property-management companies, like Rockport Holdings. Now, normally you might link Rockport only with swank properties in the financial district, banks and such, but you'd be wrong. They also own blocks and blocks of low-rent units throughout the city, many bought up on spec for redevelopment, which makes Rockport the biggest slum landlord in town. But I tell you, each time one of their dudes in a suit comes in, say, to go over the accounts, old Beaton's all smiles and handshakes. He ushers the suit into his office, gives him the best chair, hollers at Cass to make a fresh pot of coffee. To us, he's about as cordial as an alligator.

Cass is all right though. She's got her hang-ups, and she has some pretty goofy ideas, like fancying up the work environment of Beaton Enterprises. One time she brought in a lot of plants that were supposed to create what she called *ambience*. Like I said, she's down to one scrawny old spider in a plastic pot. Another time she baked fudge brownies for the personnel.

That's Jaco and me. Jaco said they tasted like burned rubber, and Cass got really mad. I said, *no, really, they're good* and even had seconds, but Jaco didn't. But the thing is, you can talk to Cass. She listens. And even if she's always telling me to smarten up, go back to school, do something with my life, she's a decent person with a good heart, as my mom would've said.

Sometimes when I have time to kill between targets, I hang around the office, drumming my heels on the floor and hitting on Cass in a casual kind of way. If she's not busy, she has me read out loud to her. Practice makes perfect, she says. Mostly she ignores me because she has work to do. She does it with one hand on the phone or keyboard and the other fishing out caramels from this tin box with a lid she keeps on her desk. Sometimes I ask if she wants to go for a beer after work. She shakes her head and says, "Keno, get serious." She's always telling me to get serious. "And would you stop doing that?"

"I am serious," I say. I quit with the heels and swat at a few flies. A man in motion, that's me.

She's never said yes yet, but I get the impression she's thinking about it.

One day I'm tossing a Ping-Pong ball from hand to hand, and I'm describing this great movie I saw on TV to her.

"It's about these guys on a raft who try to outwit a submarine."

"A raft outwit a submarine? Pretty uneven odds, wouldn't you say?"

"That's how life is," I tell her. Seriously.

She gives me an eye roll and gets on with tacking up a poster on the wall behind her desk and then another like it in the front window. It's for a guy named J. Morgan Stone. He's a city councilor. You can't help knowing about him. He's always in the news, he and his mother, who's big on the social scene. He comes from money, and he's running for city mayor. I can tell by the care Cass is taking with the posters that she's got a thing for this Stone character. I miss my catch, and the Ping-Pong ball rolls under a table. I leave it and go outside to help her line up the second poster. This J. Morgan character is good-looking, if you like the smarmy type—big toothy smile, with just that touch of gray at the temples. He's holding his hands out in front of him, and underneath it reads: *The Future Is In YOUR Hands*. Like he's giving the future to you, and like you have a choice. And if you believe that, you'll believe anything.

"Is it straight?" Cass yells at me through the glass.

I step back, make a frame with my fore-fingers and thumbs. "Down on the left. Bit more. Perfect-o." I direct her so the poster is actually slightly crooked.

"What's with this JMS dude?" I ask when I go back inside.

"J. Morgan Stone," she corrects me as she sits down at her desk and starts shuffling through some papers. "He's the man who's going to clean up this city. Reduce crime. Put an end to violence against women. He's our new moral beacon."

"Ooh, he's gonna keep us on the straight and narrow?" I ask.

"My uncle is donating to his campaign," Cass says, very huffy. "And I'm volunteering at his headquarters, taking calls, handling donations. But with the election coming up in two weeks, I start canvassing door-to-door for him tomorrow night."

"Hey," I say. "I'll come with you." It's a chance to be with Cass outside of the office.

She laughs. "No thanks. I have a better offer. J. Morgan himself. I'm his sidekick. While he does the talking, I hand out the

25

flyers, take down the names of folks needing rides to the polls. I can't believe my luck. Do you know he's the most eligible bachelor in town?"

"I have the inside track on him—his mommy doesn't let him out on his own." I'm lying. I don't have any track, inside or outside. But judging by what I've heard, his *mother* should be running for mayor, not him. I shrug. I get enough of the door-to-door stuff anyway in my job.

"I hope you're going to vote for him," Cass says.

"Uh, yeah," I say. Not likely. I've already taken a strong dislike to him. I say, "Well, maybe we could go for pizza after."

She sighs, shakes her head and reaches for a caramel. "You don't give up, do you?"

I grin. Persistence—it's a word I just learned how to spell—wins the day, my girl.

I'm crawling around on the floor, looking for the Ping-Pong ball and wondering about politics. I'm not political. I know you're supposed to do your civic duty, that in some countries they have to fight for the right to vote, but as far as I'm concerned, one party is as bad as the other. The only things that are different are the slogans. I'm thinking how corny this *Future Is In Your Hands* thing is when the inner-sanctum door opens, and to my surprise, who should step out but the owner of the hands himself? He was in there all the time. Beaton was probably writing him a fat check.

I push up too fast, bang my head on the underside of the table with a loud crack and meet the floor again. Beaton glares at me like I'm scum, Cass stifles a giggle, and I feel like a total jerk. But JMS, on his way to Cass's desk, flashes a wall of dental enamel and never even breaks stride. He takes her hand and says, "I want to thank you for all the help you've been giving us, Cassandra."

Cassandra? What kind of a name's Cassandra?

He says, "Well then, see you tomorrow night. Five o'clock?" And old Beaton chimes in, "I'll make sure she's there, JM," as if Cass—excuse *me*, Cassandra—can't be trusted out on her own. I see the look she gives him back—JMS, not her uncle— like the man's just granted her caramels for life. Like she'll never wash the hand he just touched. Pure hero worship. Keno boy, I think to myself, you got competition.

I crawl out from under the table in time to watch her and Beaton wave the tooth prince out the door. He disappears into a black Lexus that's parked at the curb despite the No Parking sign. There's even a traffic warden writing out a ticket for the beat-up Toyota next car down. But JMS just nods, the warden touches his cap, and JMS gets in his shiny car and drives away. Above it all, know what I mean?

Beaton turns and glares at me. No smile, no handshake. "What are you hanging around here for, Kalder? Why aren't you out there chasing deadbeats?"

I'm about to say something very rude but Cass is there, so I say, "Waiting for my ride." Which is true. Jaco is supposed to pick me up at the end of the day, which is the start of ours.

Cass goes back to her desk and gets to work. Beaton goes into his office and slams the door.

At four Jaco turns up, and we set out. Our first call is old Mrs. Walter, who happens to be on our way. I collect from her every month. She's one of those who pay up regularly but don't mail checks—they just need someone coming around. She's a nice old bird, is Mrs. Walter. Sometimes we chat. She always has her money ready, a lot of it in loose change, but this time she won't even open the door.

"How do I know you're not the Hammer?" she yells at us from inside. "I tell you, no one's safe around here anymore."

Like everyone, she's spooked by the killings.

I say, "Hey, Mrs. Walters, you know me." I put my face where she can see me through the peephole. "Do I look like the Hammer?"

"No," she grumbles. "But how do I know? With all these goings-on, how does anybody know?"

"Tell you what," I say. "You just put your money in something, a plastic bag or something. Me and my buddy here will walk away. You open the door real fast and throw it out—" She yanks the door open and pokes me back with her cane.

"Take it," she says and shoves it at me, a handful of bills and coins. I count it, write a receipt and give it to her. All the while she's holding me at bay with her cane, like I'm a tiger or something. "Can't trust anybody," she says and slams the door.

I hear the lock turn, the rattle of a chain.

"Jeezas!" Jaco wheels around like he's seen everything and storms back to the car.

We have a quick conference as we drive, because the rest of our calls won't be as easy. In fact, our next stop is Amber Light. It's a week later, and knowing how sly she is, we're teaming up and timing our visit for when we think she'll be getting home from work. Although with Amber it's a little hit and miss because, as I told you, she's a cocktail waitress and her schedule changes. It's a useful strategy, catching people just as they're walking in the door. It's a lot harder for them to slam it in your face or pretend they're not home. And it's funny—even deadbeats, especially women, don't like to make a scene in public. They'll yell at you from inside the house, but not outside in the hall or on the sidewalk, where the neighbors can hear. Sometimes they'll even give you what cash they have on them just to shut you up. That's what Jaco calls the psychological approach.

But it doesn't work with Amber, because when we pull up in front of her duplex, she sees us before we see her. Or before Jaco sees her. I've already spotted her Corolla nosing around the corner. She brakes and makes a fast U-turn. I don't say anything, but the U-turn tells me she hasn't got the rent. Mr. Movie Producer, or whatever her big opportunity was, didn't come through. We park and get out. Jaco takes the front door and points me to the back. That way he thinks we've got her covered. I go, give it a while, jingle change in my pocket, do a little two-step in place just to pass the time, then stroll back to the front. I stand by real casual while Jaco leans on the bell.

"Guess she's not in," I say. Talkover? Heck, I'm Mr. Walkover where this lady is concerned.

Now Jaco's hammering on the woodwork with his fist.

"She's screwing us around," he snarls, blaming me for another dud call. It puts him in a nasty temper for the rest of the evening, which maybe isn't a bad thing because our targets get the message he's not in the mood. By eight we're done for the night, and we're batting four out of five, which is eighty percent, up fifty points!

FOUR

Jaco's yelling at me as we drive back to base.

"I told you a million times, dumbbutt, you hook 'em, you reel 'em in. There's no such thing as *next week*!" Amber really has him stewing.

I say, "So she's working nights. Or she's visiting her mom in Windsor. And don't call me dumbbutt."

He gives me a hard look. "What's with the mom in Windsor?"

I sluff it off. "Personal profiling." We're supposed to keep it strictly business with our targets, no getting friendly. We're the heavy artillery. But developing a personal profile on them is different if it helps us track them and produces a payout. I put the mom in Windsor under personal profile. But Jaco is suspicious.

"Ah, you poor sucker, you been chatting her up?"

"No," I say. "And lay off with the *poor sucker* bit. Anyway, what's the big deal? We'll get her next time."

He slams on the brakes so hard I nearly choke on my seat belt. He says through his teeth, "The hell with next time. She's paying up *now*." And he swings a right and heads across town to the Azure Club on Simmons. Now *that's* personal profiling. It's another of Jaco's techniques. Know where they work and catch them at their place of employment. It's a card you have to play carefully, however, because you can get thrown out. Or some employers get so freaked they fire the target, and then there's no hope of ever getting money out of them. But Jaco's so mad, he's ready to blow the thing apart. He's yelling and swearing and driving like a lunatic. I let it roll off me. I'm not worried. If Amber is smart—and she is—she'll be lying low.

It takes the Azure Club bouncer plus the bartender to convince Jaco that Amber isn't there and he's wasting his time. Jaco doesn't let on that he's the rent collector, lets them think he's an angry boyfriend, and me, I'm there for moral support. Better that way. When he finally storms out of the club, he's smoking.

"Listen." I pile into the car beside him. "Call it a night, okay?"

"Shut it!" he hollers. "I've had it with her. *Nobody* jerks me around like that." He's out for blood, and he accelerates back across town in the direction of her duplex.

All I can do is fold my arms and sit tight. I know she won't be at home, but I hope for her sake she'll be able to come up with the back rent the next time we find her. I've done everything I can for Amber. Jaco mad can be really ugly.

It's now almost nine, and it's a repeat of our earlier call. Jaco takes the front, I take the rear. This time, to my surprise, there's someone home. A radio is playing softly. And there's a crack of light showing through the kitchen curtains. How I know it's the kitchen is I've been there often enough. I've stood on enough garbage cans and rain barrels and deck furniture, looked through enough windows, to know the entire layout of just about every house we call on. Apartments are different, but with houses and 'plexes you can usually manage to work out the floor plan. It's especially important when you're dealing with sliders like Amber.

Just then I see the curtains flick, so someone's checking to see if the coast is clear. I grin and step onto the porch, positioning myself at the back door but keeping an eye on the windows too. I'm almost enjoying myself. I hop around a bit to keep warm. The night has a chilly edge to it that reminds you winter's on its way. Apart from the radio, everything is still, which makes me wonder. The state Jaco's in, he should be kicking in the door, knocking the furniture aside. So she must have let him in because she doesn't want a scene. No raised voices, either, so maybe he's calmed down and is talking reasonably with her. Or maybe, just maybe, she's counting out twenties.

I stay where I am, shifting from one foot to the other because standing still is hard for me. Next thing, I hear a shout. I'm not too sure where it's coming from or if it's really a shout. Could as easily have been the bark of a dog, or the hoot of an owl, if they have owls in the city. Then I hear a noise inside the kitchen, and I brace myself. If Amber is on the run, I'll scoop her up as she comes out. She's a little lady, hardly an armful. I'm not prepared for the door to burst open like the Calgary Stampede. It catches me square in the chest, and I go flying backward. I land, roll and fling myself after the figure rushing past me. The light from the open doorway is enough for me to see that it's not Amber. Shit, it's not even a man. It's Dracula, tall and black, with a dead-white face and slick, shiny bat wings that rustle as it flies past. It scares me so much that I miss the grab and wind up snatching air. But somehow I feel I ought to know the face.

Of course, it isn't Dracula. It's some guy in a black plastic rain cape who's in a real hurry. He's gone. I don't bother chasing him. He's not the target. Then the face comes back to me, and for a moment I'm stunned. It's the tooth prince, J. Morgan Stone, but this time he definitely wasn't smiling.

So what's a dude like JMS doing running out of Amber's house? I have a pretty good idea what he was doing *in* her house, and in the next minute I laugh, because I also realize why he bolted, not like Dracula but like a rabbit. I'd run from Jaco too if he came blasting in, mad as a bull, while I was cozying up to a chick. Or maybe a candidate for mayor and a moral beacon doesn't want to be caught hanging out with cocktail waitresses. Personally, I've got no problem with it, but it's the kind of thing that might not go down well with the voters.

The back door is practically off its hinges, old JMS came through it so hard. I stroll in, expecting to see Jaco putting the pressure on Amber. But the house is strangely quiet. I go through the kitchen into the hall. The hall light's not on, but there's enough of it coming from the kitchen for me to see Jaco standing just inside the front door. He's looking down at something. It's Amber, sprawled flat on her back, and she's wearing some kind of dark scarf that's fanned out around her hair.

"Shit, man," I say to him. "I know she pissed you off, but did you have to sock her?"

When he doesn't answer, I move in closer. That's when I see that the scarf is not a scarf, and Amber's face isn't much of a face anymore. It's an open wound, and what I thought was a scarf is blood that's collecting in a pool around her head. I'm walking in her blood.

Someone's yelling, and I realize it's me. "What the hell did you do to her? What did you do?"

Jaco reaches across and slaps me hard. I blink and stagger back.

41

"Is she dead?" I whisper. "Did you do this?" I want to throw up.

"What do you think?" His voice comes out as a croak.

"What d-do I think? I think you k-killed her." My tongue's so tied up I can hardly get the words out. "You s-stupid SOB, you hit her and she's dead. It's why you like this lousy job. So you can shove p-people around, beat them up. You really get off on this kind of thing. Well, you sure did it this time!"

He hits me again, and my nose spurts blood. I turn to run, but he's on me, slamming me against the wall. I think of the Shadow.

"I didn't do it," he's saying. He has me by the shoulders, his fingers twitching as they dig into me. He's shaking. *I did not do this!*"

But I know he did. In the six months I've worked with him, I've seen how he likes roughing people up. I've seen him get

42

a bit more violent each time. I hate a bully. I always have. And I realize, in that moment, it's why I've never liked Jaco. I can picture it. Amber hardly has a chance to open the door before he crashes in. He was steaming when he left the Azure Club, and he's venting all his rage on her. She's a small woman—her bones are fragile. All it takes is one blow from his massive fist to cave her skull in.

"It wasn't me!"

"If it wasn't you, who was it?" I shout back.

He lets go of me, and his shoulders slump. "I swear, I did it by the book. I rang the bell. I knocked. But the front door wasn't locked. So"—he hesitates—"I came in." That's *not* by the book. Although we do it, we're not supposed to enter uninvited. He makes a strange noise in his throat. "She was like this when I found her. I damn near tripped on her." Now he wipes the back of his hand over his eyes. "I heard a noise. Someone was in the house with her! He took off out the back! You must have seen him!"

Yeah, I saw him. He knocked me on my ass. It takes me a minute to get my head around it. J. Morgan Stone?

It takes Jaco a moment, too, to understand what I'm saying. "You mean the guy who's up for mayor?"

I nod.

"You're sure it was him you saw him running out the back?"

I nod again.

He thinks. I can practically hear his brains whirring. "Why was he wearing a rain cape?" he asks.

I shake my head. "Dunno. Maybe he was expecting rain and didn't want his Armani suit to shrink."

"Come on," Jaco says. "We gotta get outta here."

I say, "We gotta call the cops. And—and an ambulance."

"You crazy? She's gone. Nothing you can do for her now. You call the cops, they'll hang it on us. They're looking for a serial killer, or have you forgotten?"

"She was dead when you found her. I can vouch for you."

"Oh yeah? And what about you? Your blood is everywhere, man. *Her* blood is on your shoes. Who's gonna vouch for *you*?"

It's true. I'm tracking it everywhere. My nose is dripping gore. I try to staunch it on my T-shirt front. It's *my* footprints they'll find, *my* blood spattered all over a crime scene. And only Jaco's word that it wasn't *me* bashing Amber's head in while he was outside leaning on the doorbell.

I don't remember leaving. I don't remember getting into the car and speeding away.

I don't remember Jaco pulling up somewhere and cutting the engine and the lights. But I do remember sitting in the dark, the sound of his harsh breathing. And I remember him turning to me and laughing, a high, crazy laugh.

"J. Morgan Stone! Who'd've thought it? Keno, baby, this could be our lucky day!"

F!VE

Our lucky day? I don't see anything lucky about it. Jaco is talking, talking. I can't understand what he's trying to tell me.

"A hundred thousand?" I parrot back stupidly. "What are you talking about?"

"One and five zeros, baby. That's fifty apiece. Just to start with." Jaco's laughing so hard the whole car shakes. "Can you beat it?" He traces headlines in the air and says in a phony voice, "Mayoral frontrunner arrested for brutal slaying. Charged in connection with Hammer murders. Now who'd want that? Who wouldn't pay up?"

"Are you talking about b-blackmail?" I fight my stammer down. "If you're talking about blackmail, you're on your own." I slip my seat belt and start to get out of the car.

"Whoa, hey, not so fast, my man." Jaco grabs my arm. "You're forgetting the alternative."

"Oh yeah, what's that then?"

"The alternative is you doing life for a crime—a whole slew of crimes—you didn't commit. Your DNA's all over back there."

"Well, if mine is, so is yours," I remind him, just in case he thinks he can strong-arm me into going along with this crazy scheme of his. "Fingerprints on the door or one lousy hair is all it takes to put you inside her house. You probably stepped in her blood too. And who got pitched from the Azure Club? Who acted like an out-of-control asshole?" I do the headline bit, complete with voice. "Man kills girlfriend in jealous rage. Club employees testify."

"Okay," he says, like it doesn't matter. "Have it your way. We both sit around until they take us down. That what you want? A cell with your own toilet for life? That what you want, huh? How long do you think it'll be before Chipmunk Cheeks makes the connection and hands us over to the cops? She's already looking at us funny. By tomorrow she'll be on the phone." Now he does a squeaky voice that doesn't sound anything like Cass's. "Oh, officer, I think I know who killed that woman."

My legs are out of the car, but I don't go anywhere. Anyone with half a brain can see the fix we are in. We may as well have left our IDS at Amber's house. She was on our hit—I mean, our *client* list. All of the murders were committed in the inner city, *our* territory. We work the area door-to-door on a daily basis, we profile targets, we stalk them, we look in windows. You don't have to be a genius to join up the dots.

Okay, so I tell the cops I saw J. Morgan Stone coming out of Amber's house. He could just as easily turn it around and say *he* saw me. It's his word against mine. The man's no dummy. He'll find a way to wiggle out of it. He has power, money, for sure the best lawyer in town. No doubt he's pals with the police chief. Crap, he's even buddies with the traffic warden. Jaco and I are bottom feeders. Who's going to win? Who's going to lose?

Chances are good JMS is going to get away with murder. Maybe a string of murders. The thought makes me boiling mad. I don't care about the money. Money's not going to give Amber her life back. I think of her with her hair done up, eyes dancing, tricked out in spike heels and that tiny, tiny skirt, perfume hanging in the air. Then I think of her lying like a smashed doll on her front-hall floor. She didn't deserve to die like that. I want the creep to pay.

If I can't lock him up, maybe bleeding him is the only way.

I pull my legs back in, shut the car door and sink back into the seat. "Okay," I say shakily. "How're we gonna do this?"

—

We talk—or, as usual, mostly Jaco talks. He says, "The odds are in our favor, man. Stone knows we can put him at the scene. He knows all it takes is a single hair. That's our ace in the hole. Plus there's the psychological factor. Even if we can't prove anything, what candidate for mayor wants to be suspected of being the Hammer?" He's good at psychology, is Jaco.

The first problem is how to get to JMS. It's easy enough finding out his phone number and where he lives, an up-market address over on the east side of town. But will he be home? Will he deal?

Our second problem is, we don't have a lot of time. Someone's going to find Amber's body tomorrow or the next day. When she doesn't turn up for work. Or when the mother in Windsor calls and gets worried because her daughter's not picking up the phone. Someone will go looking for Amber. And when they do, we need to be gone from this town. Shit, I think. Did we remember to close the front door? Did I leave the back door open? Did the neighbors in the duplex hear me yelling?

Our time frame suddenly shrinks to hours. What Jaco said is true. It won't take Cass long, or old Beaton for that matter, to figure out that Amber was one of ours. And that we paid her a little visit tonight. And that if someone left her with only half a face, it probably was us. The Azure Club boys will remember Jaco coming after her, and me the backup. They'll ID us easy. Suddenly, getting the money from Stone and splitting becomes extremely important. We argue over should we call him or drive over to his house. It's safer if he doesn't know who we are. We decide to call. Or Jaco will call, because I'm not good under pressure.

I think of something. "What if you get voice mail?" I spend my life talking to voice mail.

So we work out what Jaco should say. It's not easy. With a recorded message, we have to be careful. We have to get our point across without landing us in you know what if JMS decides to take it to the cops. Finally, Jaco is satisfied with the wording. Next, we dicker over whose cell phone we're going to use, because neither of us wants the call traced back to us. We flip for it, I take tails, it comes up heads, and Jaco makes the call on my phone. It rings at the other end, and someone answers, but it's not Stone. Jaco's not fazed. He's quick on his feet, is old Jaco.

"Good evening," he says, real smooth. "Is Mr. Stone available? He's not? Oh, you're his mother. Well, I'm real honored to be talking with the mother of this great city's next mayor."

He laughs, and I gather from his laugh that Mother Stone appreciates his wit. Then Jaco says, "Listen, sorry to disturb you, Mrs. Stone, but it's about your son's campaign. Well, it's a funding opportunity, but rather than bother you with it, why don't I just call back, you let voice mail kick in and I'll leave a message? But be sure to tell him to listen to it as soon as he gets in. It's very important."

She's okay with that, and Jaco hangs up. See what I mean about quick on his feet?

He calls back a few seconds later. When voice mail comes on, Jaco clears his throat. "Mr. Stone, your presence tonight was noted. We think you'll make a good mayor, and we'd like to help. But it's a question of visibility. What people see and don't see.

We think a donation of $100,000 might be appropriate. Call us back at"—Jaco looks at me. I tell him the number. He finishes with, "Don't delay. This offer is time limited."

Jaco disconnects and puts the phone on the dashboard, and now we sit back and wait. Or Jaco sits back. Me, I'm hunching forward and staring at the phone so hard it makes my eyes ache. When the phone rings about ten minutes later, I'm so wired it nearly sends me through the car roof. Without thinking, I grab it, hit *Answer* and shout, "Hello?"

Right away I know I shouldn't have done that. Like I said, I'm not good under pressure. My mind gets gridlocked. I can't spin things out like Jaco. But it's too late.

"What's this about?" Stone hisses. He got the message, all right.

"One hundred g-grand," I stammer. "We saw you. We know what you did. We need the m-money tonight."

"Are you crazy? Who the hell are you? You saw nothing. You can prove nothing."

I hear the fear in his voice, and it gives me a sense of power that lasts for half a second before Jaco snatches the phone from me.

"Listen, Mister Mayor-to-Be, it's simple. The money *now*, in unmarked bills, or you're history. You heard. One hundred grand. Or what? Or we blow you open. Proof? All we have to do is put you at the scene of the crime and let the lab boys go to work. They'll find something of yours. A fingerprint, a hair, a flake of skin—that's all it takes. And then there are the other murders. Think how embarrassing it'll be for your mother to discover her son's a serial killer. How disappointed your supporters will be."

Stone has a lot to say. Jaco listens for a bit. He laughs and sneers, "Rich dude like you can lay his hands on more than that.

And no, we don't take checks." He listens some more. Then, "It'll do for a down payment. But you got less than two hours. Downtown bus terminal. Rent a locker. Bring the cash in a briefcase and leave it in the locker at exactly 11:30. If you're one minute late, the deal's off. Then go to the men's room downstairs. Wash your hands. Leave the locker key on the sink counter under a paper towel. Walk out. Don't look back, don't even look sideways, and don't try anything tricky. You won't see us, but we'll be watching you. And Mr. Stone, just so you know, your I.O.U. on the balance is only good until 6:00 PM tomorrow. We'll call you with further instructions."

JMS has said he can come up with ten thousand cash. It's as much as he can put together in the time we've given him. Half of ten is five. I'm good with that. We head straight to the bus terminal to scope the layout. I'm wound up tighter than a spring. I want to get this over fast. Jaco says, "Relax. Just think of him maxing out every credit card he has, burning up every ATM in town. That should make you feel good."

How're you supposed to feel good when your insides are jumping out of your mouth? There's no parking near the terminal, so we have to leave the car a couple of blocks away. Jaco digs around in the trunk, pulls out a ratty gym bag and strolls off, swinging the bag. Just another traveler. He thinks of everything, does Jaco. We walk into the terminal an hour ahead of schedule.

Funny thing is, what we're doing isn't a lot different from staking out a target. You operate as a team, work to a timetable, case the entrances and exits, think out your moves, anticipate theirs. It's getting late, but the buses are still running, passengers arriving and leaving. Which is good. It gives us cover. There's a big waiting area with rows of seats. Across from them are the lockers. At this time of night, plenty are available.

Here's the plan. We pick a spot where we have a good view of everything. Closer to the time, I get up and position myself near the top of the stairs leading down to the toilets. We both know what Stone looks like—me from a close encounter, Jaco from the posters. As soon as Stone shows, I head to the men's. If there are other guys down there, I mix with them. If not, I hide in a toilet stall and wait for him to come in and leave the key. I nip out, grab it and follow him up, but not too close. I pass the key to Jaco and tail Stone for a bit to make sure he really leaves the station. Oh, and I forgot to say, I have Jaco's car key, because once out of the station, I keep going. I get the car and drive it to the curb, like I'm picking up a passenger. Jaco scoops the money, leaves the terminal and jumps in, and we head straight to my place, which is only three blocks away. Then we divide the money and work out a plan for the big drop and pickup next day. Tomorrow we call Stone with the new instructions. I try to imagine ninety thousand cash. Old JMS is going to need to bring it in a suitcase.

It's now a quarter to eleven. Forty-five minutes to go. Jaco gets us some coffee and a couple of donuts.

"Energy, my man," he says.

We sit in the waiting area. There's something crazy about stumbling on a freshly dead body, setting up a blackmail scheme, preparing to meet the killer and trying to swallow a donut, in that order. It sticks in my throat, but Jaco's cool with the whole thing. Me, I'm spilling my coffee and checking my watch every twenty seconds. My feet are dancing on the floor, my eyes are darting here and there. Again I feel like puking but manage to hold it down. Jaco seems to enjoy my stress. His superior smile tells me what he thinks of me: a dumbbutt who isn't up to it. I'm not sure I trust him, but like it or not, we're in this together. He can't cheat me without re—re—my mind's so boggled I can't find the word. Oh yeah, repercussions. I don't care about the money. I almost don't care about Amber anymore, I'm that scared. I just need enough cash for a one-way ticket out of here.

Maybe to calm me down, Jaco starts talking about himself. It really surprises me. Up to now he's never breathed a word about his private life. Far as I know, he hasn't got one. First he starts in on how fate has dealt him a bad hand. Makes him sick how all these fat cats with their college degrees are pulling in big bucks, driving fancy cars, living the good life. While he's trawling the bottom. He's smarter than a lot he can name. Just never had a break. But that's all going to change now. He's practically rubbing his hands over the money to come. Then he tells me something that makes me stare as if he's suddenly grown a second head. I quit twitching, it knocks me back so much. Turns out he has a wife and two little kids. Six months and three years old. He gets a little soppy as he talks about them, how he wants them to have a better childhood than he had. Shit, who would have thought a tough bastard like him had an ounce of feeling?

At 11:15, Jaco stands up. Time to move. He shifts forward a few rows, sits down next to a couple of women and chats them up. As I stroll past, I hear them say something about going to Thunder Bay to see a friend who's having a baby. He acts real interested. You have to hand it to him.

He even manages to look like he's traveling with them. But he's simply placing himself closer to the lockers. I go toward the stairs and hang out there. I don't see Stone. But then, at 11:26, I see him coming through the revolving door. He's in a hurry, his hair's not so smarmed down anymore, his tie's crooked, and he's looking really rattled. He's heading for the lockers. I make eye contact with Jaco and head down.

There's one old guy in the men's when I go in. He finishes at the urinals and leaves. Now it's just me. I slip into a stall. My watch says *11:29*. I picture JMS opening a locker, stowing the money, coming downstairs. I get the bright idea of getting up on the toilet seat so my feet don't show under the partition. Let him think the place is empty. And in case you're wondering, yeah, at this point I'm nearly crapping my pants.

I'm feeling pretty antsy by 11:34. By 11:40 I'm wondering what's taking the tooth prince so long. By 11:45 I'm feeling something has gone wrong, but I don't dare leave because it's up to me to get the key. By 11:50 I'm in a sweat and sure there's been a screwup. I slide out of the men's, looking both ways. There's no one coming down the stairs. The only person in sight is a janitor wheeling garbage down the hall. I take the steps in twos and do a quick scan of the waiting area. There's a scattering of passengers walking through the terminal. A group of tired-looking backpackers. Two old women dressed in black carrying what looks like all their personal belongings in cardboard boxes tied with string. There's no one at the lockers. No Jaco. No J. Morgan Stone.

It takes me a moment to realize I've been double-crossed. But I'm not sure by whom. Did JMS somehow manage to give us the slip? Did Jaco take off with the ten thousand, my half included? Before,

I was worried. Now I'm just plain mad. I race out and down the street to where we parked, expecting to see empty space, because of course Jaco has a duplicate car key and of course he's taken off without me. Funny thing, his car's still there. So where's Jaco? I do a quick run back through the terminal, looking every- where. He isn't there. Stone isn't there. Neither, far as I can tell, is the money.

SIX

sit in Jaco's car, trying to calm down, get my breathing under control, work out what to do. My first impulse is to drive to Jaco's, catch him before he takes off with my half of the cash. I'll tell him what I think of him, a slimeball, a double-crossing bastard, shout it out in front of his wife and kids. Problem is, I don't know where he lives. He knows where I live because he's dropped me off a couple of times, but I know next to nothing about him. Apart from what he told me about his family and all, he's like a clam. I claw around in the glove compartment, in the sun visor and side pockets of the car, looking for something, anything, with his address. Zilch. I'm not even sure what his last name is.

My next impulse is to go home, pack what I need and take off. I don't have much money, but I've got Jaco's car and I can disappear. Then I think maybe going home isn't such a good idea, because I'm starting to wonder, What if Jaco *didn't* double-cross me? He has a temper like a bear, but somehow he's never struck me as the kind of guy who'd go behind your back. He'd sooner smash your face in. That makes me think of Amber. I wish I hadn't used those words.

So let's just say the tooth prince showed up as instructed. Say he cooked up a convincing story and brought the cops with him. They nabbed Jaco. Then why didn't they get me? I can't work it out. But no matter how you look at it, our little blackmail caper has been blown sky-high. We're on the hook for Amber's murder, and for all I know, the cops are staking out my pad.

The only place I can think of to go is Cass's, which is on Bergmann, at the other end of town. I know, not because she's ever invited me over, but because one time I followed her home. I didn't mean anything by it. I was just curious to see where she lived—a condo development with bushes out front in a decent neighborhood. She has the ground-floor unit. It's a lot nicer than my place—an old three-story house rented out by the room with a shared toilet and shower on every floor and a communal kitchen in the basement. It's actually not too bad. The landlady, Mrs. Sousa, keeps it pretty clean. And the rent is reasonable, especially for this city.

It's now past midnight, and Cass, as you can imagine, isn't happy to see me when she finally comes to the door. She's wearing a terry bathrobe over blue pajamas, her face looks kind of naked because she has no makeup on, her hair is full of curlers, and she's wearing some kind of pink frilly cap. At first she thinks I'm drunk and refuses to let me in.

"Please, Cass," I beg. "I'm in big trouble here, and I didn't do it. I swear I didn't do it!"

"Didn't do what?" She opens the door a little wider, and I push in. "What happened to your nose? There's blood on your shirt. Have you been in a fight?"

It all pours out of me. I watch her eyes go wide when I tell her about Amber. She puts her hand over her mouth. "Oh my god, you're talking about Amber Light? I know her—knew her." She gropes behind her for a chair. "She works—worked at the campaign headquarters with me. In fact, I was a little jealous of her because I thought she'd caught J. Morgan's eye."

"She caught more than his eye." I watch her disbelief when I tell her about JMS. But I don't tell her everything.

She says, "J. Morgan Stone? Are you mad?" Then she says, "You're pacing like a caged animal. Sit down—you're making me dizzy. I'll fix you some tea. And tell me again what happened."

She goes into the kitchen, and when she comes back the cap and curlers are gone, but her hair still holds the shape of the curlers. I don't drink the tea, but I go over what happened once more with her. She sits very quiet, listening like she's trying to make sense of it. Finally she says, "I want to believe you didn't kill her, Keno. But J. Morgan Stone? That's impossible. Do you know who he is?"

"Yeah, the Hammer," I say.

She yells, "He's running on a platform of law and order, for God's sake. He's the man who's going to come down on crime in this city. He's promising to get guns and drugs out of neighborhoods, to give women back the night. He's the only candidate who cares enough to campaign in the inner city, to shake the hands of the down-and-outers, to listen to their problems. How could someone like that be a serial killer?"

"I saw him, Cass." I'm pleading with her to believe me. "He knocked me down coming out of her house. We practically caught him in the act!"

"But there could be a perfectly innocent reason why he was there. I told you he was a little sweet on Amber. Maybe he's been seeing her."

I think about Amber's hot date.

Cass adds a little sadly, "She was very pretty." Then her face goes harder than I've ever seen it. She pulls her bathrobe around her tight. "Has it occurred to you that it could just as well have been Jaco?"

"What?"

"You don't know what happened in that house. You were around back, you say. Okay, maybe Stone *was* with Amber. They might have been working on campaign business. There could be a hundred reasons why he was there. But Jaco's another story. I've never liked him. I've always sensed a violent streak in him. You said he was out of control when you went back to her house. What if she answered the door and he hit her? Maybe he didn't mean to kill her. He just lashed out and hit her."

I'm shaking my head. "He couldn't have done that much damage with just his bare fist, Cass. You weren't there. You didn't see her face, the blood."

"So who's to say he didn't use a hammer? Her eyes narrow as her suspicions grow. "Oh, God, who's to say he doesn't *carry* it around with him?" Her voice is rising. "There are four dead women, all with their heads bashed in, and the police are looking for a serial killer. If you ask me, Jaco's more likely to be their man, not J. Morgan Stone. I think you should go straight to the police. Tell them what you told me."

"I can't." Now I have to explain to her about my blood all over Amber's front hall, her blood on my shoes, my bloody footprints. But I don't breathe a word about our blackmail scheme. "Even if the cops find proof that Stone was there, Cass, *we* were there too. It's our word against his. Who are they going to believe?"

"You, if you tell them the truth. That you weren't actually with Jaco at the time. That when you went in you found him standing over her, and she was dead. Let the police draw their own conclusions."

She has me doubting now. And it's not something I hadn't already thought of. Jaco definitely has an anger-control problem. He's violent, and he's always putting people down. And yet...Call me a fool. I don't like him any more than Cass does, but he's not the kind of guy who'd sell you to save his skin, and I don't want to do it to him. Honor among SOBs.

"I better go," I say.

"To the police, I hope," she says.

I stand up. It's no good. She's got it in her head that Stone is innocent, which makes Jaco guilty. Either him or me, and I guess I should feel flattered she hasn't pinned it on me. "I gotta get out of town, Cass."

"Running will only make things worse. It's like admitting you're the killer."

"What can I do? Sharks like Stone are king of the sea. Bottom feeders like me never win."

"Keno—" she begins, but I cut her off.

"Just do me a favor, Cass. You're going to hear about this sometime soon. Give it a couple of days, okay? Before you turn us in. Will you do that for me?"

She looks at me, blinking back tears.

"Wait," she says. She runs out of the room and a minute later comes back, stuffs a wad of fives and tens into my hand. "It's all I have. You're going to need it."

Her eyes are wet and worried and kind. I would have died for her in that moment.

SEVEN

It's now 2:00 AM and my thinking is this. First I drive past Amber's street. If there are no flashing lights, no crime-scene tape, no uniforms, it means they haven't found her. Then I drive by my place. If it looks quiet, I go in, pack my gear and get the heck out. As I cut across town, I try to think of where I can go. I've got no family—my mom died when I was seventeen, never knew my dad, no brothers, sisters, relatives. No real friends. I mean, I'm *it*.

Amber's street is dark and quiet. My street is quiet too. No cops on the sidewalk, no SWAT team on the roof. I have to park down the block because there's no space out front. As usual, someone's left the front door of the house unlocked. The land-lady, Mrs. Sousa, is on us about it a lot, but tenants are always coming and going. Some work shifts. Others keep irregular hours. We figure each of us locks his own room, so what's the problem?

The first thing I notice is that *my* door isn't locked. In fact, it's open just a crack. This could mean one of two things. It might be that Loopy Luis has been on his rounds again. Every now and then he gets hold of Mrs. Sousa's keys and lets himself into people's rooms. He never steals anything, just likes nosing around. The only reason Mrs. Sousa doesn't kick him out is he's a bit simple and he's her son.

Or it could mean someone who *isn't* Loopy has been in my room. By now my skin is crawling. I listen, take a deep breath, push the door back slowly with one finger. It's dark inside, and the light from the hall isn't enough to let me see much, but I can make out something that makes my hair rise. Someone's sitting in my armchair. The light from a streetlamp outside my window outlines the shape of his head. I start to bolt, but a hoarse cry stops me.

"Keno—"

"Shit, man!" I almost explode with relief. It's Jaco. I flip the switch and nearly die of fright again. He's sitting crookedly, clutching his left arm, and there's blood seeping out of him, almost as bad as Amber.

"What the hell? What happened?"

The story comes dribbling out of him. Stone put the briefcase in the locker like he was told, but Jaco made the mistake of standing up too soon. He was only trying to move closer, but the women he'd been talking to yelled out, *Hey, you forgot your bag!*

He'd left it on the chair. That made Stone turn around. Their eyes locked for a second, but it was all Stone needed. Jaco thought he could still pull it off by picking up his bag, saying goodbye to the women and strolling real casual out of the terminal, like he really was leaving. But Stone had tagged him. Instead of going down to the men's, he followed Jaco out, caught up with him, rammed a gun in his back and pushed him into an alley.

"Call your friend," he says.

"What friend?" says Jaco.

"I know there are two of you. Get him here."

"The money first," Jaco tells him.

Stone laughs. "For your information, the only thing I put in that locker is newspaper. I'm not as stupid as you think. Now call your friend."

"And what?"

"And we talk. I'm not looking for trouble, fellow. I'm sure we can come to some arrangement."

Jaco trusts him about as much as a starving hyena. So he makes a show of digging out his phone but whirls around and slams Stone with his bag. Stone goes down but gets a shot off, hits Jaco in the shoulder. Somehow Jaco manages to get away.

"He's after us, Keno," he croaks. "He means business."

"Oh great, so you come here?" There are red, wet splotches on my floor. I'm sure a trail leads right up to my door.

"Where else"—he's shivering, and his words come out jerkily—"could I go?" I can see he's almost fainting. His face is paper white. I'm wondering how much blood he's lost.

"We got to get you to a hosp"—I start to say.

"No!" he coughs out. "No hospital. No doctor. *Please*." Never in all the months I've worked with him have I heard Jaco say please. It comes out as a long, shaky sigh. *Pleeeze*.

"Well, then we gotta get you home."

He says even louder, "No!" He's hanging onto consciousness by his fingernails. "Not safe…wife…kids…" He pulls his phone out, speed-dials, pushes it at me. He wants me to talk to his wife, tell her to pack up the kids, get out of town. I take the phone. She answers. I tell her who I am. She senses right away that something's wrong.

"What's happened? Where's Jaco? Is he all right?" Her voice is soft but scared.

"Sure," I say and stop. I'm a rotten liar. What do I tell her? Everything's cool except her husband is maybe dying?

Jaco mutters, "Jeezas" and grabs the phone back. "Honey, don't ask questions.

Just take the kids. Go to your mom's. No, trust me. Go! *Shit, will you just do it?*" His voice is shrill, but he packs everything into those few words—worry, caring, anger, fear.

He disconnects, the phone drops from his hand, he passes out. At this point I hear a sound that makes me freeze—someone has just opened the front door. Like everyone else, I left it unlocked. Now my heart is in my throat. It could be one of the other tenants. Or it could be Stone. All he had to do was follow Jaco's trail. I push my door shut quietly, turn the bolt, jam a chair under the knob, yank the curtains closed, lean against the wall, suck in my breath. Footsteps go up the stairs. Next thing, I hear them creaking overhead. I let air out like a leaky balloon.

I have a look at Jaco's wound. It's a big red mess. I'm no medic, but I do what I can. I get some scissors, cut away his shirt. It looks like the bullet entered his left shoulder from the back and went on traveling out the front. The hole is jagged, like a flower. I pull off my T-shirt—it already has my blood on it—and press it against him to stop the bleeding. I don't like the way he's breathing—really wheezy. His skin is cold to the touch. I'm afraid he's going to die. I grab my phone, start to dial 9-1-1. His *Please* echoes in my ears. I put the phone down, get a blanket, cover him up. His color is really bad, kind of a fish-belly white.

"Oh shit, man," I say. "Don't go out on me."

I realize my teeth are chattering. I hunt for another T-shirt, put it on and my hoodie over that. Then I turn out the light and sit there in the dark. It feels safer that way, and it's easier not seeing him. But I can hear his shallow breathing over the thumping of my heart. I remember I was planning to skip town. I can't leave him, but I don't know how I can move him. And somewhere out there, Stone is looking for us. With a gun.

So now you know the beginning of my story, and we're back at the middle, where you came in. And you know why before the night is out I may be dead.

EIGHT

I pull out my cell phone. It glows green in my hand. I hesitate before hitting the automatic dial for Cass. She's in my phone memory, partly because it makes me feel good having at least one frequent-contact number and partly because I call her sometimes when I'm feeling down. She never seems to mind. This time I'm not feeling down. I'm shit scared. But I'm not sure she wants to talk to me anymore.

She doesn't. I don't wake her up because she hasn't been able to get back to sleep since I was there, but she's plenty upset to hear from me again. I guess she hoped I was already gone, out of town, out of her life. It takes some persuading, but she calms down enough for me to tell her about Jaco.

"So do you believe me now?" I ask.

"I believe he got into some kind of trouble, and you're covering for him." Over the phone I can't see her expression, but her tone is as stiff as a board. "You're saying J. Morgan Stone killed Amber, shot Jaco and is now coming after you? This gets crazier and crazier. How does he even know who you are?"

"He knocked me down, remember?"

"And you gave him your address?"

"We—we talked to him, Cass."

She squeaks, "You *talked* to him? You think he's a killer and you *talked* to him? What's going on?"

Now I have to tell her about our black-mail attempt. For a minute there is silence. Then she explodes.

"How could you, Keno? How could you do it? A woman is brutally murdered, and you two"—she searches for a word—"you pieces of *scum* try to turn the situation to your advantage by blackmailing a perfectly innocent man?"

I tell her it wasn't my idea, that I didn't want to do it. Stone isn't innocent. I explain the bind we were in. Halfway through my explanation, she hangs up.

I kill my phone, drop to the floor and sit there in the dark with my head in my arms for I don't know how long. My thoughts are jumbled like the pieces of a jigsaw puzzle. I try to block out the sound of Jaco's breathing. I want to forget he's there. I guess I must doze off, because somehow I'm running down a long, narrow alley, and JMS is coming up behind me with a gun. He's spraying bullets that kick up dirt all around me and ping off the brickwork. And then, looming in front of me, is a high, high wall. There's no way I can get around or over it, and I think, This is it, Keno. This is what your whole stupid life comes down to. A dead end. I turn, and the tooth prince is there, smiling, his teeth as big as windows, the barrel of the gun pointing right at me. I yell, "This is no dream!" He says, "Goodbye, chump" and fires.

The sound blows my ears out, but it's only a light tapping noise. I nearly jump out of my skin. Another tap. Then a voice.

"Keno. It's me. Cass."

I struggle up, go to the door, but I don't open it. "Are you alone?" At this point I'm sweating and shaking and trusting no one.

"Of course I'm alone," she hisses. "Let me in."

I drag the chair away and open the door a crack. She pushes her way inside, swinging something hard that knocks me in the knee.

"Did anyone follow you? How'd you know where I live? " I'm as nervous as a scalded cat.

"No one followed me, and why shouldn't I know where you live?" she snaps. "You're personnel. I deal with your file every week. Why are we talking in the dark?"

I hit the light and see she's carrying a big bag.

"Oh god," she moans when she sees Jaco. She rushes to him. "Is he—is he—"

As good as, from the look of him. His color has gone from white to doughy gray.

She pulls a first-aid kit out of the bag and gets to work on him like some kind of Florence Nightingale. She peers at the wound, makes disapproving noises. She gives me orders, tells me to boil water, to support him so she can clean him up front and back, dabs at him with cotton pads, sprays on antiseptic. Jaco is conscious now, mumbling and trying to fight her off.

She says, "Shut up and sit still. You're seriously hurt. If you're too stupid to go to emergency, then I'll have to tend to you myself. Don't think it gives me any pleasure. If it weren't for Keno here, I'd leave you to bleed to death. Which is what you're going to do in about two minutes if you don't stop moving!"

He does as he's told. He looks so much like a kid sent to the principal that, in spite of the shape he's in, I almost laugh. She packs the wound with gauze pads, then binds everything up. Together we help him to my bed and put the blanket over him.

My place is just a room. Besides the bed, I have an armchair, a table, two chairs, a lamp, a portable TV, a mini-fridge and a microwave. That's it.

Cass and I sit down at the table.

"Will he be all right?" I ask.

"He's too pig-headed to die," she says.

"He's got a wife and kids," I say.

"I don't know how she stands him."

"He's not that bad." I'm not sure why I'm defending him.

"If you like rattlesnakes," she says.

She's giving me this look that has me squirming, like she's weighing her options: does she help me, or does she throw me to the cops? She sighs, drags the bag over. I get to see what else she has in it. Her laptop, a manila file and what she calls an accounts ledger and we call a rent book. Hoo boy, I think, she's nuts. She's bringing work from the office here? She pulls the file out. In it are newspaper clippings on the murders. She's been collecting them. She lays them out on the table.

"I did some research and found out where the first three victims lived. " She takes out a piece of paper with addresses written on it.

"Now, look at this."

She pulls out the laptop, keys in something, and a city map pops up on the screen. She rattles away on the keyboard, typing in the murder addresses, and all three come up as red dots. They're concentrated in the north half of the inner-city zone. It takes me a minute. Then I get it. Jaco's patch.

I almost laugh. "You saying Jaco's a serial killer? Those women were on his list?"

"He wouldn't be that stupid. But it *is* his territory."

"Yeah? Well, it's mine too, when we work together, which is pretty often. Or are you saying we're into tag-team murders?"

"Don't be ridiculous. But there's something else you should see."

She flips the rent book open, runs a finger down a page and keys in a few more addresses, which show up in blue. The red and blue dots lie all mixed up together.

"I don't get it."

"I'm saying, Keno, the blue dots *are* on Jaco's list. They're tenants he regularly collects from. Their locations lie very close to the places where those three women were killed. Jaco's in that area what, weekly? Several times a month at least? He passed by the victims' addresses all the time. He could have noticed those women on his rounds, targeted them. He might even have chatted them up. And Amber, of course, he knew."

"Aw, c'mon, Cass. I worked Amber too. And anyway, Jaco doesn't chat people up." But then I think of how easily he got friendly with those chicks at the bus station.

"How do you know? How do you know what he gets up to when you're not with him? Think about it, Keno. The killer had inside information on his victims. He knew things about them. Where they lived, that they lived alone, when to find them home. He knew *them*. And they knew *him*.

93

The locks weren't jimmied, the windows weren't smashed. The victims let him in. Maybe *you* don't want to believe Jaco did these terrible crimes, but *I'm* saying he fits the murderer's profile a whole lot better than J. Morgan Stone does!"

I have to chew on this for a moment.

She sees the look I give her.

"Okay, just tell me one good reason why you think J. Morgan is a better suspect"—she jabs her chin in the direction of the bed—"than *him*."

"I'll give you three," I say. "One, Jaco can get nasty, but he's no killer." I say it, but she has me wondering. Those blue and red dots are dancing in my head. "Two, Stone's face is on every poster in town. Hot-shot candidate for mayor, campaigning door-to-door. Great opportunity to target victims. And who wouldn't welcome him in? Three, I caught him leaving Amber's house."

"I told you, he could have been there for a perfectly innocuous reason." She glances quickly over at Jaco, but he's out cold. She lowers her voice anyway. "And I still say you only have his word for it that Amber was dead when *he* went in."

"Then why would Stone cut a deal with us if he's so innocent?"

"He doesn't want to be associated with a horrible murder. Can you blame him? He's a candidate for mayor, for God's sake."

"Shooting Jaco's going to send him to the top of the polls?"

"He didn't mean to. He just wanted to make you guys see reason. And maybe it was Jaco who pulled the gun, they struggled, and it went off accidentally."

I shake my head. "Accidentally on purpose. Your boy Stone killed her, Cass. He's trying to silence us. You're just too in love with him, too stubborn, to see it."

Now the look on her face turns mulish. A she mule with its ears laid back, ready to kick.

"I am *not* in love! And *you're* too stupid to see what's right in front of your nose!" She bites off the words, snaps her laptop shut, puts it and the rent book in her bag, grabs her first-aid kit, stands up.

"I'm finished here," she says on her way out. "I've done all I can for him"—again that chin shove—"for both of you. You asked for a couple of days. I'll give you until they find Amber. Once her murder is in the papers, I'll have to take this information to the police. I'm sorry, Keno. It's not that I want to get you arrested, but I'm already in this deep enough. You're making me an accessory to murder. And extortion. That means blackmail, in case you didn't know."

She stomps out. I follow her into the hall. Before she reaches the front door, she turns and says, "And another thing. I am not your mother, Keno, or your problem fixer, or your anything. Don't call me again."

She's gone.

I go back in my room. Shit, I think. Now what?

I see that Cass has left the news clippings. I look through them again, reading slowly. I always thought serial killers went for a certain type. Apart from the fact that the victims, including Amber, lived alone in low-rent housing, they didn't have a lot in common. Their ages were twenty to forty. Their hair was blond, black, brown. They were short, fat, tall. Amber was a redhead, little and slim. Not even the dates fell into a pattern. You know, like every full moon. The first murder was in March. The second in July. The third in September. And now, with Amber, October.

I'm not sure what I'm seeing. And then I get it. Four months, two months, one month. *The killer is picking up the pace.*

NINE

"Jaco."

He groans but doesn't wake up. I stand there, looking down at him. His forehead is bunched up like a fist. Even passed out, he looks mad at the world. I don't know. What if Cass is right? Maybe JMS was only having it on with Amber when Jaco burst in. Stone took off because, like Cass said, he didn't want to be caught messing around with one of his campaign workers. He has a socialite mother. He has an election to win. Or maybe he went to Amber's house, found her dead and ran.

Who wouldn't run? He agreed to pay us not because he killed her but because, like Cass said, being linked to a murder inquiry isn't a good campaign strategy. Did he really shoot Jaco? Or was Jaco lying? Why would he lie? Questions bounce around in my head like numbered balls in a lotto draw.

The money. It's the only reason I can think of. Ten thousand reasons. I remember how Jaco couldn't wait to get his hands on the cash. Maybe the gun *was* his. Maybe he tried to up the ante with JMS, they struggled, and it went off. It makes a crazy kind of sense. And maybe Jaco *is* behind the murders. The victims lived in his territory. As a collector he'd know how to stalk them. And he knew Amber. I start pacing. My head is spinning.

Get a grip, I tell myself. I wish I'd never got Cass involved. She has a way of complicating things. I have to make some choices, and there's only one way to do it. I start to shake Jaco awake, but I don't want to grab his wounded shoulder, so I end up slapping him lightly on the cheeks.

"Listen, man, and listen hard," I say when he finally comes to. "I want the truth. You lie to me, I'm outta here, and you're on your own. What really went down with Stone? Did he shoot you, or did you try something with him?"

He's pretty groggy, but he manages to croak, "Are you crazy? How was I gonna try something when he had a gun? It happened like I said."

"And Amber. Did you really find her like that? Or did—did you hit her?"

"Shit, man, I never touched her!"

"What about those other women?"

"What other women?"

I come right out with it. "The other three. *Are you the Hammer?*"

He pulls away from me like I've got some kind of disease. "Ah, jeezas, now I know you're nuts."

"Cass thinks it's you. She's worked out that all the victims lived in your territory. She thinks you stalked and killed them. She thinks you murdered Amber."

"You believe that?" His voice is high, almost a squeal.

"I believe you're one mean SOB."

He manages to sit up, using his good arm. His face twists with pain. "Listen, dum—" He checks himself. "You know how deadbeats piss me off. Sure, sometimes I rough them up a bit. Comes with the job, man. But I don't punch their lights out. They're standing when I leave them, aren't they?"

I think of the Shadow, of the hundred shadows he's banged against walls. I guess banging's not the same as punching. And yeah, they're all still on their feet when Jaco finishes with them.

He goes on, sounding really offended, like I spat on his manhood or something, "And I don't beat up on women. You ever seen me even lay a finger on one, hey? Much as I want to for jerking me around, you ever see me do that?"

The answer is no. He yells, he swears, he threatens, but I've never seen him touch a woman. I remember the catch in his voice when he told his wife to get out of town with the kids.

"So whaddya think, dumbbutt?" He comes out with the word this time, and somehow I don't mind. "Do you believe me now?"

"Yeah," I say. I don't tell him how close a call it was.

Okay, I know where I stand with Jaco. This still leaves me having to work out a plan. I check my watch. Almost five. It's dark outside, and right now darkness is my friend. There are bloodstains. On the side-walk, up the front-porch steps, down the hall, leading right to my door. Once it gets light, all Stone has to do is follow the trail.

And if he doesn't get us, the cops will. As soon as Amber's body is discovered, Cass will turn us in. It's clear she worships JMS, and she'll do anything to protect him. The cops are looking for a serial killer. It's just a question of who finds us first. Them or Stone.

"Okay, buddy," I say to Jaco. "I know you're in no shape to travel, but we got to make a move."

I pack a few things and drive us out of the city in Jaco's car. Jaco slumps in the passenger seat, nursing his bad shoulder, grumbling at every pothole we hit. What a wuss. At this time in the morning, there's very little traffic on the road. I'm not sure where we're going—just following our headlights north. By seven it's growing light, and by eight I see we're already into farmland, fields of stubble waiting for winter, and every now and then sad clumps of trees. We stop at a roadside diner offering all-day breakfast and endless coffee. Jaco doesn't want to go inside with his arm all bandaged up, in case someone asks questions. I brought the blanket with us, so I throw that over him.

"Act like you're cold."

There are no customers in the diner. The cook, a big fat man, is sitting behind the counter reading the morning paper. While we give him our orders, I squint at the headlines. *Mayoral race intensifies.* Something about the NFL. Nothing on Amber. We order ham and eggs, pancakes with syrup, toast, hash browns, a gallon of coffee. Jaco eats everything in sight, which tells me he's feeling better.

Jaco says it's time we figured out where we're going. When we get back in the car, he digs out a map, studies it for a bit and picks a spot on the edge of a lake in the middle of nowhere.

"Why there?"

"It's fishing country. We find an isolated cottage and break in."

"Then what?"

"We hang out."

I see us hanging out, like, forever in some fisherman's cabin with winter coming, no heating and outdoor plumbing.

So it's back on the road. We leave the main highway a little after ten. Now we're winding along on small side roads through heavy forests, with lakes popping up all around us. The next time we stop, it's for gas. The station has a small café tacked on to it. Jaco puts the blanket on again and we go in. He's already interested in lunch. He orders coffee, a sandwich and a slice of coconut cream pie. I just have coffee. After that big breakfast, I'm not hungry. I count our money. Emptying our pockets and with what Cass gave me, it comes to $108 and change.

"Not going to get us very far," says Jaco with his mouth full.

"When we run out of money for gas, we can—" I almost say "sell the car" but realize right away that'd be a great way of helping the cops trace us. Dumbbutt, I tell myself. "Walk," I say instead.

It's funny how my mind jumps around. Suddenly, I'm thinking of the endless streets Jaco and I have walked together. How we've made our way between garbage cans and chained-up dogs, hopped over rotten steps, banged on doors with their screens torn off. And I see myself still doing this rotten job a year, three years, six years down the road. Then I remember my dream, the dead-end alley, and I'm scared again. Not because Stone is chasing me, but for a different reason. I'm scared I'll end up like Jaco. I don't want it, man. I really don't want it.

And then—because it's the way my crazy mind works—I think of Cass. Cass walking. Canvassing door-to-door. With J. Morgan Stone.

I stand up so fast I knock the table, spilling Jaco's coffee.

"What the—" he starts to say, but I talk over him.

"We gotta go back." Already I'm heading to the cash register, my wallet out.

He catches up with me, blocks my way. "Are you nuts?"

The waitress is looking at us like she's afraid we're about to start a fight.

"It's Cass," I say. "She's in bad trouble. Or will be in less than five hours."

TEN

I'm speeding back the way we came, and Jaco's yelling at me to turn around. As soon as Amber's body is found, Cass will blow the whistle, and we're dead meat. I'm shouting about Cass's canvassing date with JMS this evening. About Amber being one of the volunteers at his campaign head-quarters. About my hunch that the tooth prince is stepping up the pace of killings.

That shuts him up. I can hear the gears turning in his head.

"Stress response," he says at last. "Pressure of the campaign gets to him, he lashes out."

Jaco sees psychology in everything. But he's on board now, speed-dialing Cass's number on my phone.

"Come on, come on," he says, but she doesn't answer. He calls the office. Beaton picks up, and Jaco immediately hits *End Call* because there's no way he wants to explain to old I'll Beat On You why we won't be in for work. Also, he remembers—we both remember—that today is Thursday, and on Thursdays Cass has classes. She doesn't come in to work until the end of the day, and because she's supposed to meet JMS at five, she might not show at all.

By now we're a good four hours' drive from the city. Then three. Then two. I'm mashing the gas pedal, pushing Jaco's old car as hard as it will go. Jaco keeps trying Cass's number. She doesn't answer. Every time he gets her voice mail, he passes the phone to me. He doesn't leave the message himself because there's no way she wants to hear from him.

"Listen, Cass," I holler, "call me as soon as you get this. It's really important. And stay away from Stone!"

Lakes, forests, fields flash by in reverse order. When we reach the edge of the city, it's four thirty, and we're into rush-hour traffic. I slam the steering wheel with the palm of my hand and say, "Shit! She's not returning my calls because she's as stubborn as a mule. She probably zapped my messages. She's already made up her mind that JMS is innocent, and she doesn't want to hear anything else. Somehow I've got to convince her, but how am I going to do that if I can't get through to her?"

"Calm down," says Jaco. "If they're going door-to-door, he's shaking hands, doing his spiel, and she's handing out flyers—he's not going to try anything."

I say, "But after? What about after? And what if she lets slip that she knows Amber is dead? That he was seen running out of her house? She's so gone on him, she'd try to warn him. We got to find her, Jaco, and we got to get there in time!"

Question is, where's *there*? Do we go to Cass's house? To the office? Head straight to JMS's campaign headquarters? Or look for her body in some dark alley? It's now nearly five, so we decide on the headquarters, and we lose a good fifteen minutes finding it. When we arrive, there are all these people milling about. They're laughing and talking, and I judge by the mood that no one knows about Amber yet. A man in a jacket with leather elbow patches is shouting out instructions and sending people off in pairs.

"I specifically instructed all canvassers to wear a jacket and tie," he says, firing a look at us that says he dislikes more about us than just our clothes. I guess we're pretty scruffy, not having shaved for twenty-four hours. Jaco's not wearing his blanket, and with his bandages he looks like he's been in a war.

"We're not here for that," I tell him. "We just need to know where J—where Mr. Stone is canvassing tonight."

"Why?" Elbow Patches looks suspicious.

But Jaco moves in on him in that way that only Jaco has and whispers something in his ear. Instead of backing off, the man just laughs.

"Oh lord! You should have said! I'll give him a call." He grabs his cell phone, keys in a number, waits, shakes his head. "He must have it switched off. Look, he's working Grove to Sunderland, Wilson to Ramona." He points to a map taped to a wall, which shows the city broken up into different-colored areas. He checks his watch. "He'll have gone straight there from his meeting."

"Is he with someone?" I ask. "Cass—Cassandra Beaton?"

Elbow Patches checks a list. "Yes, she's with him."

"Which end would they have started at?" I say, but Jaco's already out the door.

"We're good," he says when I catch up with him. "That's my beat. I know it like my own hand."

We get in the car, and I say, "That guy laughed. What did you tell him?"

Jaco pulls a crooked grin. "Just that we're the hired help, and Stone's mommy sent us with a jacket in case her darling boy got cold." He gives me a pained look. "*Cassandra?*"

We head for the inner city. It's Jaco's beat, but I've worked it too. Which makes it seem like a nightmare where you're in a place you're familiar with, but everything looks strange because you're seeing it differently. It's growing dark, and shadows are reaching out from everywhere. Every woman we pass looks like Cass, every man like JMS. When we approach Grove, I slow down. We take it block by block, weaving back and forth between Wilson and Ramona.

We finally spot them on Henderson. I brake and cut the lights, and we watch them going from door to door. To my relief, there are actually four of them, working in pairs. Cass is with JMS, all right, but there's a man and another woman across the street. After every few calls, they meet and confer on the sidewalk. The other man points a flashlight at a clipboard while Cass writes. Then they split up again and take the next few houses on each side of the street.

I don't follow them but instead turn around and park at the end of the block one street over, and I keep doing this as they move along street by street. What they're doing is so much like my job as a collector that it almost makes me laugh. Only they're chasing votes, not bad debts.

When they finish off with Sunderland, it's past eight thirty. The four of them walk back toward us, pass by without so much as a glance and keep going. Cass is talking and laughing. I get this sick feeling in my gut, because I've never seen her so happy. We follow at a distance, creeping along with the headlights off. At the end of the road, the four of them get into Stone's Lexus. We tail them back to campaign headquarters, where Stone parks at the curb. All of them go in. About half an hour later, they come out again, but this time the other couple gets into another car. Cass is alone with JMS, and they're walking toward his Lexus.

I'm half out of the car, wanting to head them off. But Jaco grabs me.

"Wait," he says.

"For what?" I jerk free. "For him to kill her?"

"We're going to follow them, dumbbutt."

"She's in danger!"

"Just stick close. Trust me on this."

I take a deep breath. "You better be right."

I pull out behind them and cling to their tail like a burr. I don't care if JMS sees us. In fact, I hope he does. At one point we're caught at a red light, and we lose him. I'm close to panicking, but then we spot his car ahead of us, turning right on Mason. The way he's headed, I already know he's taking Cass home. This might seem harmless to you, but not to me. Every one of those women was killed in her own home, remember?

We follow them to Bergmann, and when JMS pulls up at her house, I'm all for roaring up and rear-ending him—anything to stop the awful thing I know is about to happen. But Jaco has me cut the lights and swing into a driveway a few doors down. I'm surprised when Cass climbs out of the Lexus but JMS doesn't. She stands there talking through the open door of the car. Doesn't matter that the street is lined with garbage bags piled up at curbside for pickup. She could be in a romantic movie set, the way her face is lit up with a smile, brighter even than the streetlamp she's standing under. They chat and chat. It looks perfectly innocent. Then she waves and goes up the walkway to her townhouse. At the door, she turns and waves again before going in. He drives off. I realize I've been holding my breath.

Jaco says, " Over to you, my man. The hard part's yet to come. You're gonna have to go in there and convince a woman in love that her sweetheart is hazardous to her health."

While Jaco stays in the car, that's exactly what I do. Or try to do.

117

"Why aren't you a million miles away from here?" Cass screeches. At first she refuses to let me in. She's in no mood to listen. JMS has suggested they go for a drink tomorrow night after canvassing. She's walking on moonbeams, already planning her hairdo, what to wear, and she doesn't want me spoiling her party. I think of Amber.

Cass stomps off into the kitchen. I follow, telling her about the dates of the murders. "What about them?" she snaps.

"He's stepping up the pace, Cass. Jaco thinks the stress is sending him over the edge."

"Jaco?!"

"I mean, first he's a city councilor, now this—this mayor thing. Maybe he never wanted it, any of it. Maybe it was all his m-mother's idea." My stutter is back, and I'm making a hash of it. Jaco could've explained it better, but I already know what she thinks of his opinion. "Whatever." I push on. "His next m-murder won't be a month from now. It's going to be tomorrow night!"

She claps her hands over her ears. "I'm not listening to this. I want you to leave right now." And she shoves me hard in the chest and keeps on shoving until I'm out her door.

Jaco says as I climb back into the car, "Sent you packing, huh?"

I'm in a sweat. "She's got a date with him tomorrow night. She's already hearing wedding bells. She can't see the danger she's in."

"Too pig-headed, that's her trouble."

"What're we going to do?"

"You've done all you can. Maybe by tomorrow she'll see sense. It's time to worry about our own necks. I got a wife and kids to think of."

"We can't just leave her, Jaco."

"'Fraid you got no choice, my man."

We argue like this, back and forth. Finally Jaco loses his temper and shouts, "Listen, dumbbutt, you want to hang around, you can. I'm gone."

I yell back, "Yeah, and how you gonna drive with one arm?"

"You'd be amazed what I can do with one arm."

"Then do it." I'm so mad I could punch him. I jump out of the car.

He climbs out too, gets in the driver's seat and peels off, leaving me standing on the sidewalk.

"Jerk!" I yell. "And I told you not to call me dumbbutt!"

All of a sudden I'm shaking, and I realize how tired I am. Tired from no sleep, tired of death, tired of blood, tired of running. I don't have anywhere to go but home. I start walking toward the subway, which is three blocks down the road. I'm almost there when a dark car turns onto

Bergmann up ahead of me, coming my way. It passes with that quiet swish that pricey cars have. It's a Lexus.

ELEVEN

I'm sprinting, even though I know I can't get there before the Lexus does. I see its taillights grow smaller in the distance. Its brake lights flare as it reaches the stretch where Cass lives. Then it moves on, disappears into the night. My legs are still pumping, but my mind stands still. Not JMS? Not his car? I'm seeing things?

My foot is on the bottom step of Cass's porch when her front door starts to open. I jump behind a bush. A minute later Cass comes out, manhandling a couple of garbage bags. As she carries them to the curb, I slide like a cat from my cover, nip up the steps and slip inside while her back is turned. I don't care if she gives me hell when she comes back inside and finds me in her house. If I can't convince her about JMS, if she kicks me out, I'll camp on her porch. That way I know she'll be safe at least overnight. I'll work out what to do about Stone in the morning, when my brain fires up again.

I'm waiting in her front room, organizing my scrambled thoughts, when I hear her laugh. I take a quick peek through the front window. She's standing on the sidewalk, talking to someone I can't see because of the shrubbery. Another laugh. This time it's a man. He says something about rain, and I recognize the voice.

Sometimes the simplest things escape me. Parking on Bergmann—on any city street—at night is next to impossible. He had to find a spot to leave the car, and then he walked back. Or maybe he didn't want to park his Lexus near Cass's place, where it could be seen.

Now they're coming in. I flatten myself against the wall. Her living room is small—you couldn't swing a cat in it. There's no place to hide. But they don't come in here. They go straight into the kitchen. And I hear him say, "No thanks, I'll keep it on for now. But I want you to know I had to come back. I couldn't stay away. Tonight calls for a celebration, Cassandra. God, I love the name. It's so *classical*."

I can almost see the flash of all those teeth.

She laughs some more, and then he says, "No, I mean it, you're an excellent campaigner. One of the best. You have natural flair for it. I could really use a person like you by my side."

"Oh, J. Morgan!" She's eating it up. I never thought a smart chick like her could be so dumb.

"There's only one little thing. I hope you don't mind my mentioning it. Your dress. It's a bit flashy for what we're all about, don't you think?"

What's *he* on about? Far as I can remember, she's dressed nice—slacks and a jacket because it's cool outside, but nothing over the top or sexy.

"I'm—I'm sorry, J. Morgan," she stammers, sounding really puzzled.

"Or maybe it's not your dress as such, but the way you come on to people. Don't think I haven't noticed how you've been pushing yourself at me since we first met."

"I never—I mean, I didn't think—"

"But it's important to *think*, Cassandra. Every moment, every word you say, everything you do, you have to think, think, *think*. Work it out in advance. Never put a foot wrong. I mean, you really have to *be* all that you stand for." He's speaking slowly, like a teacher out of patience with a dimwit kid who can't understand a simple lesson. I recognize the tone because *I've* always been the dimwit kid. Not the sharpest knife in the drawer, old lightbulb not quite screwed in, elevator doesn't go up to the top. The way he's talking to her bothers me so much, I step into the hall, not caring anymore if they see me. But they don't. They're standing in the kitchen, facing each other, not looking my way. The kitchen drawers are hanging open, like she was in the middle of digging around for something. He's holding a bottle of wine, passing it from hand to hand, going on about how badly she's let him down. She's looking up at him as if he's kicked her. And he's wearing a black rain cape.

"Where's that damn corkscrew?" he shouts and thumps the bottle down on a table.

She's almost in tears. She whispers, "Sorry" and turns away to rummage in the drawers.

That's when he pulls the hammer out. He had it under the cape, and he has the cape on because a hammer is a messy weapon. That's when I yell and lunge. The hammer partly misses its target as I tackle him but still delivers Cass a sickening whack. Call me two bricks short, I don't care. I hit him with the full load.

TWELVE

Concussion. I learned how to spell it. I always thought it was *s-h-u-n*—concu*shun*, like that. Anyway, Cass has it, is still a bit headachy and woozy. She cried a lot when she came to and learned that the cops had hauled JMS off in handcuffs. He tried to talk his way out of it, tried to lay it on me, said I was the one with the hammer, even tried to get Cass to back him up. But good old Cass came through and told them what really happened.

JMS is being charged with Amber's murder and aggravated assault on Cass.

The medics say she's lucky she has a very, very hard head, or it would have been lights out for her as well. JMS is denying everything, of course, so it's no surprise that he's keeping mum about our little blackmail scheme. It opens up a whole can of worms, like if he was innocent, why didn't he report us to the cops right away? Why bring a bag of phony cash to the bus terminal? Why shoot Jaco? Naturally, Jaco and I are staying zipped too, and Cass is cool, acting like she knows nothing. Anyway, the tooth prince has a lot more important things to worry about. The lab boys have the hammer, and I don't think it will be long before they tie him to the other killings.

The papers are all over the story, I don't have to tell you. They're careful with their wording, saying stuff like *alleged killer* and *shocked, unbelieving public* and *possible psychotic episodes* and *undergoing psychiatric assessment*. I'm the hero of the day.

Got my picture on the front page. Jaco grumbles a bit. After all, he's the one who took the bullet.

"Quit grousing," I say. "You want to be charged with attempted extortion? That's blackmail, by the way."

As you can imagine, Mrs. Stone, JMS's mother, has hired the city's top criminal lawyers. She's busy pulling in favors right and left to wipe her little boy's nose clean.

They're keeping Cass in hospital another day for observation. That means someone is always coming in to take her blood pressure, shine a light in her eyes, check her reflexes. She keeps telling me to go home, she's fine, but I'm not leaving her. I brought her roses and the biggest box of chocolate-covered caramels I could find. Believe it or not, Jaco even brought her flowers.

Old Beaton doesn't know what to do with us. On the one hand, we saved his niece's life, so he has to be grateful. Cass is insisting he give me and Jaco a raise. On the other, it turns out JMS owns Rockport Holdings, which is Beaton's main account. Or rather, *was*, because Beaton just lost their business since it was his own collectors who put Rockport's top man in jail. Cass says good riddance. Not only is JMS a killer, but he's the city's biggest slum landlord, which is how he was able to pick his victims. He had access to their rental contracts, knew who lived alone and where. You can bet old I'll Beat On You is pretty sore at us. He doesn't call Jaco and me the Two Bagels anymore, but I think he'd love to zero us out.

So now you have the beginning and the middle of the story, and it's all over but the shouting, you might think. Life picks up where it left off, business as usual, Jaco and me back doing our rounds. But I have a feeling that isn't the way this story's going to end. You see, raise or no raise, I want out, and Jaco's come up with a bright idea.

He figures we're pretty good at the crime-solving business. He thinks we should form our own business, part-time at first, until we find our feet. He even has a name for it. The Triple O Private Investigation Agency.

"Bagels for sure," says Cass, and I'm not sure she's kidding. "But triple? You and Keno. Who's the third?"

"You, Cass-o," says Jaco. "You didn't do bad when it came down to the crunch. And in this game, girls can play too."